Presented to

_____

From

_____

Date

_____

Dedication

To my parents, Bill and Lois,
who taught our family to love and respect
all creatures "great and small."

Thank you for allowing us to bring home
the injured or lost, teaching us to
care for each of them.

George the Squirrel

Laura McLeod

BOOK ONE IN THE MERRY MISFITS SERIES

George the Squirrel
by Laura McLeod
Copyright ©2014 Laura McLeod

ISBN 978-1-58169-548-9
For Worldwide Distribution
Printed in the U.S.A.

Illustrated by Lisa Alderson

Evergreen Press
P.O. Box 191540 • Mobile, AL 36619
800-367-8203

Meet George...the Squirrel!

George is just an average grey squirrel who likes to climb trees, play with other squirrels, and eat all the time. But he was not always like other squirrels.

One day, when George was about three days old, he fell from his nest high in a tree. Down, down, down he went until he landed onto a pile of soft leaves. Shaking his head, he stood up and licked his paws as if to say, *That was scary, but I guess I'm all right.*

Baby squirrels are born with their eyes closed, so George could not see a thing. He felt tired and decided to lay down and take a nap. Suddenly he heard footsteps. It was a boy and a girl coming close.

"Willy, look up in that tree—it's a squirrel's nest!" Libby shouted.

"And look over there," Willy pointed, "there's a baby squirrel on top

of that pile of leaves! He must have fallen from the nest. What should
we do?"

Libby thought for a moment and then told Willy, "Pick some grass.
I'll run home and get a shoe box so we can make a nest for him. But
don't touch him. Dad told me that you should never touch a wild
baby animal because the mommy may not take him back. Wild
animals don't like the smell of humans on their babies."

Willy said, "Okay. I promise not to touch him."

Libby and Willy agreed to meet back at the same spot in a few minutes. Libby came running from the house with the shoe box and some gloves, and Willy had picked a small pile of grass.

The children decided to hide behind a bush to make sure the mommy squirrel wasn't looking for her baby.

After a long time the baby squirrel made a funny noise, "de-de-de."

And there still was no sign of the mommy squirrel.

Hearing the funny noise, Libby said, "I guess that's squirrel talk."

"I think he's hungry," Willy told Libby. "We need to do something."

So Libby put on her gloves. "I think we have waited long enough for his mommy to come get him. Let's gently lift the baby into the box. We'll take him home and ask Mom and Dad what to do."

"Mom…Dad…" the children shouted out as they entered the house. "We found a baby squirrel, and he's asleep in this shoe box."

Mom hurried from the kitchen to see what all the noise was about. Looking at her children and the shoe box, she said, "You know, kids, he is a wild animal. I'm not sure this is a good idea. He's probably hungry and scared. Your dad and I will talk about it and decide what to do." Mom headed for the family room to talk with her husband about the baby squirrel.

"I hope we can keep him. He's so cute and little!" Libby told Willy as they waited for their parents to decide.

Mom returned and said, "Children, your father and I talked about us taking care of the baby squirrel and here are the rules: We will all take care of him until he is big enough to go back outside and be on his own. We cannot forget that he is a wild animal and needs to live with his squirrel family. Genesis 1:24 talks about wild animals living together, so we need to do what's right. Your father will call the vet, Dr. D, and ask him what to do."

"Yeah!" Willy and Libby cheered and jumped for joy. They were so happy they were going to take care of the baby squirrel.

Dad called Dr. D who suggested they come by his office with the baby squirrel. Libby and Willy's little brother, Cole, was taking a nap so Dad offered to stay at home while the others went to visit the vet.

Mom, Libby, and Willy piled into the car to drive to Dr. D's office. After everyone buckled their seat belts, the children held the shoebox closely between them, as they drove to the vet.

When they brought the baby squirrel into his office, Dr. D looked him over and said he looked very healthy. He told them to feed him every three hours and keep him warm and dry.

Dr. D said, "You will need to feed him special milk with a very small bottle for kittens, kind of like a doll's bottle. I will give you everything you need before you leave."

When they got back home with the special milk and little bottle, they saw that the baby squirrel finally started to wake up! He gave a big yawn and stretched his little legs out.

Cole also was waking up from his nap and saw Libby holding the shoebox. He asked, "What's that?"

Libby explained to Cole, "Willy and I found a little baby squirrel in the woods." Cole wanted to know the squirrel's name. Libby replied, "He doesn't have a name yet."

Cole looked in the box and asked, "Can we name him George?" The whole family thought that was a great name, so George he became!

When George began making his "de-de-de" sounds again, Mom said, "I'm sure that means he's hungry. Libby, please make the special milk like Dr. D said. When it's nice and warm, pour it into the bottle and we'll try to feed George."

After Libby put the milk in the bottle, she held it up to the squirrel's lips. George took his first sip and made a squishy-icky face! He knew this was different from his mommy's milk. But he was so hungry he decided this would be okay for now and drank the milk with all his might, thankful to have something to fill his tummy.

After he ate, he soon fell asleep again. Everyone had fun taking turns feeding him over the next few days.

One morning, when he was about two weeks old, George's eyes opened for the very first time. He squealed with happiness and the children came running.

I can see, I can see...oh boyyyyy, everything is soooo big! Wow, I am soooo small! George thought.

The children saw that his eyes were open, and they were happy too. George could finally see them!

But what a surprise they were to him. They looked so strange. *Where is their fur?* George wondered. *They only have fur on their head! And no tail?* George thought how weird they looked.

The days passed and they all continued to care for the little squirrel. They fed him and played with him. George could tell they all loved him very much.

One night when Libby was rubbing his ears, she looked into his big eyes and said, "I love you, George! I know when you are older and bigger, we will need to set you free to live outside. But I will miss you so much!" After giving him one more pat on the head, she said, "Good night, George, sleep tight!"

Then Libby whispered a prayer, "Thank you, God, for George. I love him so much! Help us take good care of our sweet, baby squirrel so he can get big and live in his own tree. Amen."

As George grew, he started to climb everywhere—on the furniture, up the curtains, and down the stairs. One day, there was a 4th of July party at their home. Everyone was having a great time!

George thought, *I want to have fun too. I can hear people laughing and having fun. Maybe I could go to the party too!*

He wiggled his way out of the box they had told him to stay in during the party and went downstairs. He thought the guests would want to hold him just like Libby and Willy always did. So he leaped across the room right onto Aunt June's head. Aunt June let out a loud shriek!

Aunt Sharon fainted and then George jumped on Aunt Patty's back! George thought, *What's the matter? I'm only a little squirrel. Didn't you ever see a squirrel before?*

Mom was not happy that he had disobeyed and snuck out of his box. She said, "Oh George, now look—our guests are upset! You were naughty to leave your box. You really need to go back in there until the party is over. Sorry, George, but not everyone likes a baby squirrel on their head, even though we all love you." Mom hugged him as she carried him back to his box.

When George was almost two months old, Libby and Willy were playing with him in the family room. Libby said, "George, you sure are getting big and your tail is getting fluffy. You are so precious!"

Later that day, the children asked their mom, "Do you think we can take George outside to play for a little while?"

Mom thought it was a good idea but warned the children to watch him closely, since George was still too young to be on his own. Libby and Willy asked George, "Do you want to go outside and play with us?"

George did not know what "outside" meant, but of course he wanted to go with them. When the children took him outside, all he could think was, *Ahh, this is what heaven must be like!*

George loved being outside. The sun felt good on his face. The trees were so big, and the smell of the grass and leaves was very familiar.

Since Cole was outside too, he wanted to play baseball with Libby and Willy. Of course, George wanted to play baseball too. So George sat upside down on Cole's shoulder while he hit the baseball. When Cole ran around the bases, George hung on tight.

George was having fun, fun, fun! Then it started to get dark, and they all went back into the house.

Early the next day, George was running around the house, climbing on the curtains. He knew Mom never liked it when he did that. He tried to obey her rules, but sometimes he just couldn't help himself. Then George went to the window and looked outside. Oh how he loved being outside! That was the best. He thought *God made the*

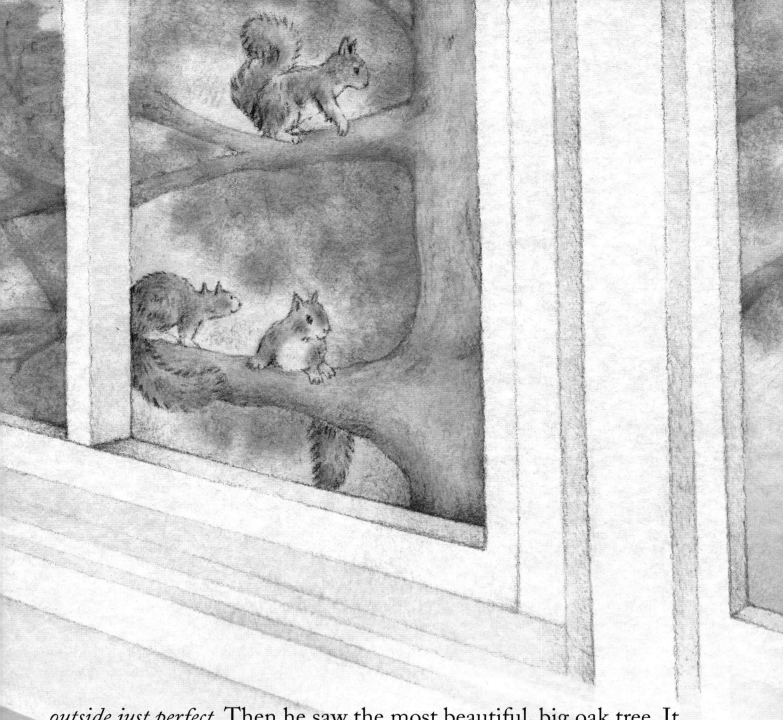

outside just perfect. Then he saw the most beautiful, big oak tree. It was huge! He wondered why he didn't see that beautiful tree when he was outside playing the day before.

He thought, *When I grow up, I want to build my home in that beautiful, big oak tree!*

Then he saw other squirrels too. There were grey squirrels with fluffy tails, running around the yard and climbing up and down all the trees!

George began to wonder if he had an outside family that looked like him—a squirrel family. He thought, *I love Libby's family, even if they are funny looking, but I want to be with my squirrel family too. Lord, what should I do?*

Dad, Mom, Libby, Willy, and Cole all knew it wouldn't be long before George would leave their family to live outside. It was the end of the summer, and George was almost three months old. The family got together and talked about George leaving them to be with the other squirrels. They were a little sad but knew it was for the best.

They all agreed that George was ready to be on his own and live in his own tree. They knew George would have a lot to do to prepare for winter. He would need to build a nest and collect nuts and acorns before the cold weather came.

The family prayed and thanked God for the fun times they had with George. They prayed for his safety and that he would keep getting bigger and stronger for his new life as an outside squirrel. Above all, they prayed he would be happy as he learned to live with the other squirrels.

Then the day came when George was ready to start his new life. One beautiful September afternoon, the whole family took him out to the backyard. George could see the other squirrels chasing each other up and down the trees. Libby gently laid him down in the soft, cool grass. He ran around the yard and thought, *This is perfect!*

Then he saw it—the beautiful, big oak tree he had seen through the window. He heard his human family cheering for him, "Go ahead, George, you can do it. Climb that tree! You are getting to be such a big squirrel, and you need to be with the other squirrels. Go ahead, George, go and be with your squirrel family!"

So he did it! George jumped onto the beautiful, big oak tree and slowly began climbing. When he got to the top, he could hear Libby and Willy cheering, "Yeah, George, you did it!"

Now George lives like a regular squirrel, but he has two families who love him! He still visits his human family every day. He climbs up to their window and watches them smile at him. He also has a nest with

his own squirrel family in the beautiful, big oak tree. The nest is full of cozy leaves, and he knows this is where he is supposed to be.

George never stopped being thankful for the children who found him and then loved him enough to let him follow his dream to live in the beautiful, big oak tree with a family of his very own.

Based on a true story!

The Merry Misfits Series is based on true stories. Each animal we have interacted with has touched our lives deeply. We found George when he was about three days old. The story is based on his time with us. We loved him. He was so funny! There are not many pictures of George, but this one is pretty good. He enjoyed veggies and peanuts very much.

Please, if you ever come across an injured or an abandoned animal, contact your local shelter, vet, or animal control officer for instructions.

Thank you to Common Sense for Animals for your love and care towards all domestic animals and for being a no-kill shelter and learning center (www.commonsenseforanimals.org). You are a great example to us on how we can teach our children.

Last, but not least, thank you to the most gifted vet, Dr. D. You are a special vet with God-given instincts and a real love for animals. We appreciate you and the lives you have touched both animal and human.

About the Author

Laura McLeod is married and a mom of two daughters who also enjoys her three stepsons. She is very proud of each of them and who they are! Laura and her family reside in Hunterdon County, New Jersey. Volunteer work has been an important part of her life, whether it is at the animal shelter, food pantry, or prison ministry. Laura enjoys the outdoors, walking and hiking, kayaking, biking, and working on her pilot's license. She is thankful for the opportunities to interact with the animals she has been involved with. Most of Laura's stories are based on one-to-one fostering or adoption of these animals.

To contact the author, visit her website:
TheMerryMisfitSeries.com

Artwork by Lisa Alderson
http://image.advocate-art.com